A/F
August 2019

ATMOSPHÆRA INCOGNITA

ATMOSPHÆRA INCOGNITA

NEAL STEPHENSON

SUBTERRANEAN PRESS 2019

First Edition

ISBN
978-1-59606-919-0

Subterranean Press
PO Box 190106
Burton, MI 48519

subterraneanpress.com

Manufactured in the United States of America

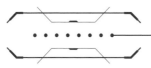

IT'S CALLED SOIL," I told him, for the third time.

Carl didn't even like to be told anything *twice*. He drew up short. "To me," he said, "it's all dirt."

"Whatever you call it," I said, "it's got a certain ability to hold things up."

I could tell he was about to interrupt, so I held up a hand to stifle him. Everyone else in the room drew in a sharp breath. But none of them had known Carl since the age of five. "All I'm saying," I said, "is that civil engineers happen to be really, really good at building things on top of *dirt*—" (this was me throwing him a bone) "—and so rather than begin this project—whatever the hell it is—by issuing a *fatwa* against dirt, maybe you should trust the engineers to find some clever way to support *whatever the hell it is you want to build* on top of *whatever kind of soil* happens to cover *whatever the hell site* you want me to buy."

Carl said, "I don't trust dirt to support a tower twenty kilometers high."

That silenced the room. With any other client, someone might have been bold enough to raise their hand and ask if he'd really meant what he said.

Or, assuming he had, whether he was out of his mind.

No hands went up.

"Okay," I said finally, "we'll look for a site where bedrock is near the surface."

"Preferably *is* the surface," Carl said.

"I'm just saying that might be tricky," I pointed out, "combined with your other requirements. What were those, again?"

"Direct access to a Great Lake," he said. "Extra points if it has a steel mill on it."

"What if the steel mill isn't for sale?" someone asked.

"It will be," I said, before Carl could.

WITH ME AND CARL it was one of those relationships where we went for a quarter of a century without having any contact at all and then picked up right where we'd left off at twelve. We'd gone to the same schools and scuffled together on the same playgrounds and even advanced as far as some exploratory kissing, which, for reasons that will shortly become self-evident, hadn't gone very well. Then the coach of the middle-school football team had refused to let me participate, save as manager or cheerleader, and my parents had yanked me out of the place and home-schooled me for a year before sending me to a private academy. This had led to college and grad school and a long dispiriting run of un- and underemployment, since the economy didn't seem interested in comparative religion majors. I'd moved to California with a girlfriend during a window when gay marriage was legal, but broken up with her before we could tie the knot—because something about knowing you *could* really focused one's attentions on what life would be like if you *did*—then met Tess and married her instead. Tess was making decent money as a programmer for a series of tech firms, which left me as one of those stay-at-home spouses with nothing to pass the time except yoga. Eventually, as an alternative to simply going crazy, I had gotten into the real estate business. I was good at all parts of it except dealing with silly home-owners-to-be who couldn't make up their minds about which house they wanted to buy.

Commercial real estate had turned out to be my ticket. Those buyers knew what they wanted and I liked such people.

People like Carl.

I'd followed his career: the cover stories in the business magazines, the photos of him opening the New York Stock Exchange. I hadn't realized that he was Carl, the kid from the playground, until he'd become a billionaire, lost most of it, and become a billionaire a second time: exhibiting a tolerance for risk that fit in perfectly with his behavioral profile during recess.

One year I'd gone home for Christmas. My mom, busy in the kitchen, had dispatched me to the grocery store to buy cranberry relish. I found myself standing next to Carl in the checkout line. He was holding a tub of sour cream and a six-pack of beer. Just me and the eleventh-richest man in America standing there waiting for Old Lady Jones (as we had known her three decades earlier) to finish coupon sorting. Carl and I had strolled across the parking lot to the Applebee's and spent a while catching up. I told him about my marriage. Carl just nodded as if to say, *Yeah, that would be you.* This created an immediate and probably stupid feeling of gratitude and loyalty that saw me through a lot of the crazy stuff that happened later.

Then some internal timer seemed to go off in his head. Maybe he sensed that the sour cream and the beer were both getting warm, or maybe that's just how guys like Carl are hooked up. He turned into a grown-up again. Asked me what I did for a living. Asked me *a lot* of questions about it, then interrupted my answers when they reached the point of diminishing returns. Requested my business card.

A week later I was back in the Bay Area. Finding Carl a hangar to store his collection of restored World War I biplanes. After that it was helping one of his companies move to a new facility in Redwood Shores. Then finding an office building for his microfinancing venture.

And it was always easy between us. Even when he was impatient or downright pissed off about something, it was always Emma and Carl, twelve years old again. Even—no, *especially*—when he came to me with a very twelve-year-old look on his face and said, "I've got a weird one for you."

"YOU WEREN'T KIDDING about the weird part," I told him, after the engineers and bankers and lawyers and a single lonely astrophysicist had all filed out of the room.

"I was going to keep it secreter, longer," he admitted, "but people can't make good decisions if I don't tell them the plan."

"Is it a plan?" I asked. "I mean, how much of this have you figured out?"

"I've had civil and mechanical engineers on it for a few months," he said, "a small team. What I haven't figured out yet is—"

"Why it makes sense?" I prompted him.

"Ah, I knew there was a reason I hired you."

HOW STEEL IS MADE sounds like the title of one of those earnest educational films that Carl and I had respectively slept through and watched in fourth grade. If you're of a certain age, you can see that film in your mind's eye: the grainy black-and-white footage, the block-letter title cards, the triumphant soundtrack trying to blow out the tiny speakers of your classroom's AV cart. Here I'm using it as a kind of placeholder for the first six months of my tenure in Carl's organization. There was no point in even starting to think about building a twenty-kilometer-high steel tower until we had figured out where the steel was going to come from.

Making no pretenses to narrative coherence, here's that six months broken down into six bullet points:

- There's a reason most of the steel mills were around the Great Lakes. These seemed to have been designed by God to support the production of steel on a massive scale. Iron ore from northern Minnesota came together with coal from Appalachia (or, later, from Wyoming) and poured into mills dotted around the shores of those enormous bodies of water. To you and me, "lake" might mean "fishing and waterskiing," but to industrialists it meant "infinitely wide superhighway for moving heavy things."

- Most of those mills were obsolete.

- The steel industry was, in Carl's unkind phrasing, "the Jurassic Park of the business world." It took a long time to pay off the massive capital investment needed to build a new mill, so owners were resistant to change. Innovation tended to be forced on them by early adopters, elsewhere in the world, who had nothing to lose.

- China was kicking the crap out of us. Most of their mills were new. They produced better product: more consistent, higher quality, easier to work with. They were getting their ore from Australia and their coal domestically. They weren't encumbered by regulations.

- None of the existing U.S. mills were making the stuff we were going to need.

- As a little side project en route to building his tower, Carl was going to have to reboot the American steel industry.

Our initial idea, which we quite fell in love with, was to plant the tower along the shore of a Great Lake and basically extrude it out the top of a brand-new steel mill. Needless to say, we got a lot of love from Chambers of Commerce in that part of the country until our structural engineers finally achieved mind-meld with some climate scientists and called us in for a little meeting.

The engineers had been getting more and more nervous about wind. It had been clear from early on that the big challenge, from a structural engineering point of view, wasn't supporting the self-weight of the tower. The amount of steel needed to do that was trivial compared to what was needed to prevent its being knocked flat by the upper-altitude winds. Kavanaugh Hughes, our head structures guy, had an effective demo that came to be known as "I am the wind." He would have you stand up in a normal, relaxed attitude, feet shoulder width apart, and then he would get to one side of you and start pushing. First he would get down on his hands and knees and push on your ankle as hard as he could. "Low-level winds," he explained. No one had trouble resisting a force applied that close to the floor. Then he'd rise up to a kneeling position, place his hands on your hip bone, and push. "Note the transfer of weight," he'd say, and he'd keep urging you to articulate what you were feeling until you got the right answer: your "downwind" leg and foot were bearing more weight, your "upwind" leg and foot were more lightly loaded. Your only way to resist the force of Kavanaugh was that differential push-pull between one leg and the other—the "couple," as he called it. "The downwind leg has to be stronger to take that extra force. But since we don't know which direction the wind might blow from, we have to make all of the legs stronger by the same amount. That means more weight, and more steel." Finally, Kavanaugh would stand up, put his hand on your shoulder, and push. It didn't take much force to knock the average person off balance. Short of that, other things were going on: not just the intensifying "couple" between the upwind and downwind feet, but some internal strains in the torso. "My trainer is always nagging me to activate my core," Kavanaugh said, "and what that means to me is a system of internal cross bracing that makes it possible for me to transfer stresses from one part of my body to another—and eventually down into one of my feet." Then he would push you until you were forced to hop away from him. "The problems are two," he explained. "First, all of that cross bracing requires more steel—and more steel catches more wind, and increases the force!"

"Shit, it's an exponential," Carl said.

"Yes, it is," said Kavanaugh. "Second, the most powerful winds aren't down at ankle height, where it's easy to resist them. They're up near the top—the worst possible place."

"The jet stream," Carl said.

"You got it. Now, I'm not saying we can't build a tower capable of resisting the jet stream. We can do anything we want. But common sense tells us to avoid places where the jet stream is powerful and frequent." He nodded to one of his new climate scientist buddies, who flashed up a map of the world showing where the jet stream wandered most frequently. And it was immediately obvious that the upper Midwest and the industrial Northeast were the worst places in the whole world to construct our tower.

Near the equator and near the poles tended to be better. Carl nixed the poles. So we were left staring at a band of latitude that, roughly speaking, corresponded to the tropics.

"I know what some of you are thinking," Carl said, after studying it for a minute, "but no, I'm not going to build this tower in some third world hellhole only to have it end up being the property of the first junta that comes along."

A few of the people in the room had actually been born and raised in what Carl considered to be third world hellholes.

Carl was oblivious. "Political stability and property rights are nonnegotiable site selection criteria."

"The northernmost capes of Australia look ideal, then," someone pointed out. And for a minute we were all ready to purchase stylish hats and join the Qantas frequent flier program, until someone in the climate science group mentioned that those areas tended to get hit by cyclones.

"Okay," Carl said, "we need a place with boring weather at all altitudes, and political stability."

The answer was the southwestern United States, with California's Central Valley being ground zero. There was quibbling. Left-leaning people denied that the United States was a politically stable entity. Right-leaners took issue with the premise that Americans really had property rights. And Californians seemed offended by the assertion that their climate was boring. People in every part of the world, it seemed, like to complain about their local weather. We began to search outward from the Central Valley. Could we find a location with better seismic stability? Better access to heavy freight transport? A nice high-altitude plateau, perhaps, so that we could get an extra height boost?

IN DUE TIME WE found promising locations in central California. Southern Nevada. Central Arizona. Southwest Texas. Every time we found a place that would work, my acquisitive instincts kicked in, and I started pestering Carl with text messages and e-mails, wanting to go in for the kill. But it seemed that all he wanted was to string these people along for as long as possible. Hoping to play them off against one another and drive the price down, I reckoned.

Then one day the following text message showed up on my phone:

Buy all 4

To which I replied:

Lol really?

And he answered:

As long as you think they can be resold without serious loss.

And, moments later:

Don't spend it all in one place

Referring, I guess, to the fact that I was about to collect four commissions on four separate purchases—and perhaps as many as three more when he decided to resell the ones he didn't want to use ("losers" in Carl-speak).

I was beginning to suspect that the tower was a ruse and that he was actually making some kind of incredibly complicated play in desert real estate.

The reality became clearer to me when Carl bought all of those properties and then began to visit those towns and show the locals the dog-and-pony show his engineers had been preparing on the subject of why it was such a great thing to have a twenty-kilometer-high tower in one's community. Lots of PowerPoint slides explaining, in the most soothing possible way, why it was impossible for the thing to fall over and crush the town. Even if it got hit by a 747.

I ended up going on many of these dog-and-ponies. I had already done the part I was qualified to do. But my job title kept morphing as the project developed. For Carl was no respecter of titles and credentials. Whomever he trusted, was in his field of vision, and hadn't said anything colossally stupid recently tended to end up being assigned responsibilities. I ended up becoming one of the advocates for this thing, completely trashing my regular business (it was okay, we worked it out in the aftermath), and had to buy a pocketbook to contain all of my loyalty program cards for Hertz, United, Marriott, et al. Then a purse to contain the pocketbook. Then skirts to go with the purse. Which I mention because I'd always been a wallet-in-the-pocket-of-my-jeans kind of girl. Tess watched my sartorial transformations with amusement and alarm, accusing me of traveling to the Intermountain West in drag. It became a little tense between us until one day the lightbulb came on and I explained: "They don't give a shit that I'm gay."

"Really?"

"Really. They actually think it's kind of cool. Most of them."

"I just thought—"

"No. The clothes are about being taken seriously." Tess was mollified, though not fully convinced.

"People are afraid it's going to fall over on them. The explanation of why this is never going to happen needs to come from someone who is not wearing black leather."

I could do the PowerPoint in my sleep. As a matter of fact I often *did* do it in my sleep, tossing and turning in my hotel bed. We'd hired a graphics firm to make a nice animated film showing the transformation of the site. Leveling the ground. Planting trees to make it purty. A new railway line, lollipop-shaped, terminated with a perfectly circular loop nine miles in diameter. Extending inward from that, the spoke lines. Half a dozen of them, one for each of the Primaries—the primary supports that would hold the tower up.

A little homily here on the subject of "why six?" In theory you could build a stable tower with only three. But if something happened to one of them—I didn't have to mention a jumbo jet strike, since everyone was clearly picturing it in their heads—the other two wouldn't be able to hold it up. You might be able to make it survivable with four, but it would take some structural legerdemain. Five was a safer bet. Six gave you even more of a safety margin as well as some benefits resulting from symmetry. The greater the number of Primaries, the closer each was to its neighbors, and that simplified, somewhat, the problem of webbing them together structurally. So six it was.

The next step was to construct the foundation strips: six reinforced-concrete tracks, each straddling one of the spoke lines. This part of the presentation went pretty fast; there wasn't much interesting you could say about pavement.

The concept of a rolling factory was harder to explain. Factories they got, but no one had ever seen one crossed with a main battle tank the size of a shopping mall. This was where the computer-graphics renderings really came in handy, showing how the thing was built from the ground up on huge steel treads, how it accepted its inputs (steel! steel! and more steel!) from the railway line that ran right through the middle of it, assembled them into trusses, connected them to the bottom of the Primary, and then pushed them straight up through a hole in the roof. It was all reasonably easy to follow, once you got the gist of it. The one part that was a little hard to convey was that each of these six rolling factories— one for each Primary—was also a structural foundation supporting its share of the tower's whole weight. The factory didn't just have to roll (slowly!) along the runway. It didn't just have to assemble trusses and feed them out its ceiling. It also had to contain hydraulic rams for pushing the tower up, transmitting its share of the weight down through its structure into the big steel tank treads and from there into the foundation strip and finally into Carl's precious bedrock.

Having gotten those preliminaries out of the way, I was able to proceed to the big all-singing all-dancing animation (complete with moving symphonic music) showing the six Struders (as we had come to call the truss-extruding factories) poised at their starting positions at the innermost extremes of the spokes, nearly touching one another. Six trains came chugging up the lollipop handle and went their separate ways around the rim line. A seventh went straight into the center, headed for a central, non-moving Struder designed to extrude the tower's core. Once each of the seven had been supplied by its own train, steel trusses—kinda like radio towers—began to emerge from the holes in their roofs, growing upward like stalks from magic beans. There was a pause as cranes went to work framing in a platform that joined the six Primaries with the core. This was my opportunity to wax poetic as I marveled over the fact that this platform would one day be twenty thousand meters above the ground, for all practical purposes in outer space, where the sky was black and the curvature of the earth visible. Honeymooners would luxuriate in pressurized suites, astronomers would gaze at the universe through glass eyes undimmed by atmospheric pollution. Rockets would launch from it and extreme skydivers would jump off.

And yet 99 percent of the workers who built it would never have to leave the ground.

The reaction to *that* was mixed. Oh, everyone understood why it made sense—you couldn't have a large workforce commuting straight up into the sky every day, breathing from oxygen tanks and swaddled up in space suits. But it did take some of the romance out of it. At some level I think that every blue-collar worker who ever attended one of these presentations was telling himself that he would be one of the tiny minority of employees who would actually get to go up high on the tower, inspecting and troubleshooting.

The rest of the movie was predictable enough. The trains kept rolling in, the Struders kept extruding, pausing from time to time so that the freshly extruded Primaries and core could be webbed together with stiffening trusses—Kavanaugh's "core muscles." We speeded up the movie, of course, once people got the gist of it. Push, pause, web. Push, pause, web. With each push the factories rolled outward imperceptibly on their tracks, moving about one meter for every fifteen meters of stuff they extruded, keeping the tower's height-to-width ratio fixed. Though, toward the end, they started moving a bit faster, making the base splay out, giving it a bit of an Eiffel Tower feel. Even the people who walked into the room claiming to be worried that it would fall over were convinced by this; it had a wide enough stance that it just *looked* stable. Up and up went the steel as I recited lore that I had picked up from Wikipedia and from meteorology textbooks and long conversations with Ph.D.

metallurgists about the different layers of the atmosphere and the varying challenges that the tower would have to contend with: down below, rain and rust. Up higher, icing. Higher yet, wind loading, the possibility of contact with a wandering jet stream (or a wayward jet). Profound cold that would render the metal brittle if we had been dumb enough to use the wrong alloys. Thermal expansion and contraction as the unfiltered sun shone on its higher reaches in the day and then disappeared at night. Each challenge was an opportunity to generate energy with photovoltaics (up high) or convection ducts (down low) or wind turbines (in the middle).

So much for the pitch.

And so much (almost) for my marriage, which barely survived all of the absences, all of those nights in chain hotels far from home, all of those alarming changes in wardrobe and hairstyle.

IF I WERE TO write a book about building the tower, I'd here interpolate a three-year-long chapter entitled "Politics and Lawyers." Halfway through it, I got a text message from Carl:

CALI = LOSER

meaning, "Sell the property in California." My response was

OK

but my reaction was a little more complicated. I had known all along, of course, that we'd end up selling at least three of the four properties. But I'd spent time in each of those places and had made friends with the locals, and I didn't look forward to breaking them the news that their bid—for by this point, each of these things had mushroomed into a complicated bid package binding together state and local governments, unions, banks, and other worthies—had been rejected.

The answer, simply, was that the tower was going to be visible from the hills above Oakland and Berkeley: a spendy part of the world where lots of rich people were accustomed to looking out the windows of their nice houses and seeing the landscape. And *only* the landscape. They didn't want their views marred by a twenty-kilometer-high "monstrosity" whose "stark, ugly, industrial profile" was going to be "cluttered" with "ungainly industrial encrustations" and "gaudy" with a "Las Vegas-style light show" that would "sully the purity of the skies night and day."

Southwestern Texas got killed six months later by environmentalists being used as sock puppets by an unholy alliance of—well, never mind. Demonstrating in court that their claims were bogus would have been expensive. Bankrolled as well as they were, they could have stretched the process out forever by filing legal challenges. Arizona was the next domino to fall. It had always been a long shot, but we'd held on to it mostly to give us greater bargaining power over the Nevada site, where local politicians had smelled money and begun to let us know, in various ways, that we were going to have to play ball.

So that was how I came to earn four commissions by purchasing four "losers" for Carl, and another four by selling each and every one of them. We made money on two, lost money on another two, and pretty much broke even on the whole deal.

That was how the project ended up where it did: between an Indian reservation and a decommissioned military bombing range, out in the southwestern desert, in an area that had already demonstrated its openness to radical transformations of the landscape, first by bombing the crap out of it, then by building a casino complex, and most recently by its wholehearted acceptance of wind farms.

At about the same time we closed a deal on an aging complex near the Illinois-Indiana border and got to work building a new kind of steel mill. The Great Lakes were still the best place in the world to make steel. This was a far cry from our original scheme to have the mill on-site. But in the intervening years it had become clear that lots of people wanted the kind of steel that a new mill could produce. Hard as it was to believe, the tower had become a minor customer.

Transportation wasn't that big of a deal. Smaller pieces could be shipped southwest on freight trains. Big stuff was barged down the river system to the Gulf, dragged through the Panama Canal, landed at the head of the Gulf of California, and then transported overland using land trains.

The site was twenty minutes' drive from a college town, which gave the employees a place to educate their kids and entertain themselves and gave us a ready supply of fresh young engineering talent.

As well as a cowgirl-themed gay bar. Which became pretty important when Carl told me—as if this should have been obvious from the beginning—that I was moving there to run the whole thing.

"I'm not qualified to construct a twenty-kilometer-high tower," I pointed out.

"Since it has never been done before," he said, "no one is."

"The engineering is totally beyond my—"

"We have engineers."

"All the legal ins and outs—"

"Lawyers."

I was dreading the conversation with Tess but she'd seen it coming long ago. Hell, maybe Carl had even prepped her.

"Let's go," was all she said.

Bless her beautiful heart, I thought. But what I said was "Huh?"

"I've been looking into it. Precleared it with my boss. I'll telecommute."

N E I T H E R O F U S R E A L L Y believed that, of course. Her job lasted for all of twelve weeks after we moved.

She cashed in some stock options and bought the cowgirl bar for less than what she had spent on her last car. With what was left over she bought a pickup truck from a rancher who had sold his land to Carl.

Five years later, the bar had morphed into *the* hangout for all the engineers, gay and otherwise, who had moved to the area.

Another five years after that, Tess was operating the First Bar in Space.

Oh, people argued about it. Space tourism had been gathering steam. Queasy/giddy tourists drifted around the tiny envelopes of their suborbital capsules and sucked pre-mixed cocktails from nippled sacs and this got billed as the first bar in space. It became like the debate on who had built the first computer: well, depends on what you consider a computer.

What do you consider a bar? For Tess it had to have a jukebox, a dartboard, and gravity. You can't get a head on your Guinness in zero gee.

At first it was just a shipping container with portholes plasma-torched by Tess's eternally grateful clientele of elite ultra-high-altitude steelworkers. This was back in the early days when the Square Kilometer—as we called the (actually round) platform at the top of the tower—was still only a couple of thousand meters off the ground. Once we broke through four thousand meters it became necessary to start running oxygen concentrators full-time, even for the altitude-adjusted regulars. On the day the Top Click (as we called the Square Kilometer by that point) pushed up past the altitude of Mt. Everest, we moved the whole operation into a pressurized Quonset hut and filled it with sea-level atmosphere. Beyond ten thousand meters we just started calling it the First Bar in Space. There was carping on the Internet but the journalists and businesspeople who rode the helirail up to the top and sat at the bar taking in the black sky and the curvature of the earth—well, none of them doubted.

I'm leaving a lot out: five years of starting the project, ten years of riding it up. Tess and I had two kids, raised them to teenagerhood, and went through a spell of personal-life hell when she had an affair with a Mohawk iron-worker who drifted in from Upstate New York and stormed out a year later when Tess thought better of it. I ran the show for a few years until Carl suddenly announced during a meeting that (a) I had done a fantastic job but (b) I was being replaced effective imme-diately and (c) he was commencing radiation therapy for prostate cancer forty-five min-utes from now. He then gave me the world's most unusual commercial real estate gig: selling off the Top Click. Obvious conflict-of-interest issues were raised by my wife's bar; Carl resolved them by giving us a lease in perpetuity, hand-scrawled on the back of a boarding pass.

Shipping materials to the top of the tower only became more expensive as it went up, so we had framed in the big structures while the Top Click had been on the ground, then stockpiled steel and other goods that could be used to finish it later. All of it got a free—but very slow—ride to twenty thousand meters. Additional structural work proceeded at a leisurely pace during the years that the Top Click was rising up through the Dead Zone—the altitudes from about seven to twelve kilometers. Below seven, humans could breathe (though most needed oxygen bottles), move around without pressure suits, and enjoy a decent enough view. It was cold as hell, but you could wear warm clothes; it was like being at a base camp on a man-made Himalaya. Much above seven, there wasn't enough atmosphere to breathe, but there was enough to supply foul weather in abundance. The view down was often blocked by clouds, the view up not yet enlivened by starlight. Past Everest height—nine kilometers or so—we got up into screaming sub-sub-subzero winds that, at their worse, were close to jet stream intensity. There wasn't much point in trying to keep glass in window frames. Even heavy-looking stuff like shipping containers had to be welded down or it would blow off, fall a few miles, and break something on the ground. There were ways to deal with it; but it basically led to Top Click operations being put in suspended animation until the Struders on the ground pushed it up out the top of the Dead Zone. During that time, we had other things to think about: sheathing the horizontal braces in giant wings, and getting them to work right.

Above the Dead Zone, things got nice in a hurry. The buildings, which had been empty shells for several years, got shelled in by space-suited workers and then pressurized with proper atmosphere so that shirtsleeved workers could get in, lay carpet, and put on doorknobs.

It was during that phase, when the Top Click was about seventeen kilometers above the ground, that we threw a party in the First Bar in Space for the purpose of scattering Carl's ashes. The basic idea being that they would fall for a couple of kilometers, get snatched by the wind, and disperse.

I was the last to arrive, carrying the guest of honor—a Ziploc bag full of Carl—in a messenger bag that looked way too hip for a middle-aged mom in the real estate business. My flight from SFO had been delayed by one monster of a storm front: the kind of thing that had been sweeping west to east across the Great Plains since time immemorial but was rarely seen in our part of the Southwest. But like the proverbial frog in a pan of water, we'd all been getting accustomed to shifts in the climate, and weather events unheard of during the previous century. The airline had found a way to route me around the storm, but as I drove in from the regional airport in Tess's pickup truck, I could see clearly enough that it was determined to catch up with me: an arc of stratocumulus anvil clouds stretching, it seemed, from Baja to Utah, blotting out the late-afternoon sun and flashing here and there with buried lightning.

It was the only thing that could make the tower look small.

One of the engineers, way back at the beginning, had described it as "a gas of metal," which was pretty poetic for an engineer but did convey its gist: the minimum of steel needed to do the job, distributed over the largest volume it could feasibly occupy, but in a specific way meant to solve a host of structural problems. At night, when the lights came on, it looked far more substantial than during the day, when it was a glinting cloud that rose up out of the desert like an inverted tornado. If you let your gaze be drawn up high enough—astonishingly high, far above most clouds—you could see its ladder of wings cruising in the jet stream, like a set of Venetian blinds hanging inexplicably in space. Above that, frequently obscured by haze and clouds, was the flare at the very top where it broadened to support the Top Click.

Even though I'd been living with—and on—this thing for going on twenty years,

I was still impressed with its scale when I approached it as I was doing now. But having Carl's earthly remains on the passenger seat somehow drew my attention to his ground-level legacy, which now spread out from the base of the tower to a radius of ten or twenty miles. Fanning away to the east-southeast was an expanse of open rangeland, inhabited only by bison, groundhogs, and a few back-to-the-land types: *vaqueros* and the Indians who had always lived in those parts. Part of it was a bombing range. The rest I had acquired, one ranch at a time, using shell companies so that the landowners wouldn't gang up on me. Because one of the questions people had asked was "What if it gets rusty and falls over?" and Carl's answer had been "Then we'll use demolition charges to fell it like a tree down the middle of the Swath," as this territory had come to be known. Which to me had seemed like bending over backward for the NIMBY types, until I'd understood that Carl had always intended to use the tower as a catapult for launching space vehicles, whose trajectories, for the first twenty miles, would pass right down the middle of the Swath, which he therefore needed to keep clear anyway so that failed rockets would have a place to crash.

The new highway from the airport ran along the Swath's northern border for the last few miles, and as I drove in I enjoyed, to the left, a vista of grazing bison and the occasional horse-riding Indian, and to the right, a generic exurban sprawl of strip malls and big-box stores that had sprung up to fill the needs of all the people who had moved here. Behind that line of development I could hear the long blasts of a locomotive whistle: another huge train rolling in from Chicago carrying prefab steel trusses to feed into the Struders.

The ring line encircling the base was discernible as a crescent of five- to ten-story commercial buildings adorned with the logos of the tech firms and contractors that had set up shop here. Mixed in were hotels and apartment buildings housing temporary residents as well as the younger, more urban crowd who wanted to be close to what had developed into a passable nightlife and entertainment district. From their windows they could look out over residential developments spreading away along the state highway connecting to the college town. All of this had a temporary feel, since it was understood that when the tower topped out and the Struders ground to a halt, the bottom kilometer would develop into a vertical city, a much cooler place to live—climatically as well as culturally.

For now, though, the tower's lower reaches were a web of bare trusses with steelworkers, and their robots, crawling about. Welding arcs hung in it like bottled fireflies, and cranes pivoted and picked like hollow mantises. In most building sites, a crane had to be capable of hoisting itself higher as the building grew beneath it, but here the cranes had to keep working their way *down* the structure as it pushed up from the Struders. It wasn't rocket science but it did make for some crowd-pleasing erector-set gymnastics, watched by vacationing families and know-it-all retirees from covered viewing platforms spotted around the ring road.

Rocket science was the domain of the innermost core, a ten-meter-diameter chimney running all the way up the tower's central axis. During the first couple of years I had pestered Carl with questions about what specifically was going to go into that empty space—that perfectly round hole at the center of every floor plan.

"You're assuming I have a secret plan," he had said.

"You usually do."

"My secret plan is that I have no secret plan."

"Wow!"

"I am going to sell—you are going to sell—that right-of-way to the highest bidder. On eBay if necessary."

"And what is the highest bidder going to put in it?"

"I have no idea. Since it is twenty kilometers long and pointed straight up, I'm going to make a wild guess that it will be something connected with hurling shit into space."

"But you really don't know what exactly?"

He had thrown up his hands. "Maybe a giant peashooter, maybe a rail-gun, maybe something that hasn't been invented yet."

"Then why did you pick ten meters for its diameter?"

"It was easier to remember than eleven point one three nine zero two four..."

"Okay, okay!"

The secret plan worked. The people who won the bidding war—a coalition of commercial space companies and defense contractors—gave the tower a shot of cash and credibility at a time when both had been a little tight.

Now cutting across the ring road, working against an outflow of traffic—workers coming off the day shift, headed home for the weekend—I passed a security checkpoint and rolled across a flyover that had been thrown across the circular railway line. This ramped down to ground level and became a road paralleling the Northwest Spoke.

Instead of paving the spokes all at once—which would have been a huge up-front expense—we had been building them just in time, a few meters and a few weeks in advance of where and when they would be needed. This made it possible to keep the paving crews employed on a steady full-time basis for years. So directly in front of the astonishing bulk of the Northwest Struder was this fringe of preparatory activity: orange flags marking the locations of soil samples, graded and tamped earth, a gray haze of webbed rebar, plywood forms, freshly poured concrete. The giant linked treads and looming hulk of the Struder rising just behind.

On the top of the Struder, evening-shift workers in safety harnesses were ascending from dressing rooms below to busy themselves on the most recently extruded truss section, inspecting, x-raying, installing sensors and lights and wires. A lot of that work had been done hundreds of miles away when the trusses were being prefabbed, but there didn't seem to be any computer-driven process that couldn't be improved upon by humans crawling around on the actual structure and writing on it with grease pencils. As the tower had risen up from the desert, data pouring in from its millions of strain gauges, thermocouples, cameras, and other sensors had given up oceans of information about how the models had, and hadn't, gotten the predictions right, creating a demand for "tweaking crews" to make adjustments to newly extruded work before it got pushed so high into the sky that it became hard to reach.

There was more than one way to the top. Climbing hand over hand had become a new extreme sport. Helipads were available at various altitudes, and work was under way to build a new regional airport at what would eventually be the twenty-five-hundred-meter level—airplanes would land and take off by flying into and out of apertures in the tower's side, saving them huge amounts of fuel as they avoided the usual ascent and descent.

Surrounding that ten-meter right-of-way in the middle were vertical elevator shafts. But the primary transport scheme was the heli-rail: a cross between a train, an elevator, and an amusement park ride that corkscrewed up the periphery of the structure, ascending at a steady twenty-degree angle. It was really just a simple ramp, about sixty kilometers long, that had been wrapped around the tower as it was built. Cut a triangle out of paper and roll it around a pencil if you want the general idea. Special trains ran on it with tilted floors so that you always felt you were on the level. Train stations were built around it every two thousand meters altitude. One of those—the second to last—had just been roughed in and was dangling there a few meters off the ground. I was able to clamber up into it via some scaffolding and catch the next up-bound train.

Actually *train* was too grand a word for this conveyance, which was just a single car with none of the luxury appurtenances that would be built into these things later when they were carrying droves of tourists and business moguls. All the regulars knew to empty their bladders first and to bring warm clothes even if it was a warm day at ground level. I shared my car with Joe, an aeronautical engineer who was headed up to fourteen thousand meters to inspect the servomechanisms on a wing; Nicky, an astronomer going to the Top Click to work on the mirror stabilization system for the big telescope a-building there; and Frog, a video producer readying a shoot about the BASE-jumping industry, which was already serving a thousand clients a year. After peppering us with recorded warnings, the car began to hum up the helirail, banking slightly on its gimbals as it picked up speed. A recorded message told us where to look for motion sickness pills and barf bags, then moved on to the more serious matter of what to do if we lost pressurization.

This was a pretty white-collar passenger manifest, but this was Friday afternoon and most of the workers were headed down for the weekend—as we could see when we looked into the windows of the crowded coaches spiraling down the opposite way.

For the hundredth time since leaving the funeral home, I reached out and patted the bundle of ashes in my bag. Carl had had a lot to be proud of and had not been shy about taking credit when earned. But I knew, just from watching his reactions, that he took special pride in having created countless blue-collar jobs. His family back home had been steelworkers, electricians, farmers. Carl had always been more comfortable with them than with the crowd at Sun Valley or TED, and when he had passed, the outpouring of grief from those people had been raw and unaffected.

As we spiraled up, we revolved through all points of the compass every four minutes or so. Views down the brown expanse of the Swath alternated with the panoramic storm front now blotting out the evening sun. The top fringes of the anvils were still afire with bent sunlight but their bases were hidden in indistinct blue-gray murk, cracked open here and there with ice-white lightning.

The car began to hum and keen as it pushed its way up into an eighty-mile-an-hour river of air. Bars of shadow began to flash down over us as we passed upward through a structure that resembled a six-sided ladder, with each rung a giant wing. For this part of the tower was not so much a structure in the conventional sense as a stationary glider. Or perhaps *kite* was the correct word for it.

The idea dated back to the very first months of the design process, when the engineers would work late into the evening tweaking their models and wake up in the morning to find long e-mails from Carl, time-stamped at three A.M. The weight of the tower—what Carl called the Steel Bill—kept growing. Sometimes it would creep up stealthily, others make a sickening upward lurch. The problem was wind. The only way to win that fight— or so the engineers thought at first—was to make the tower beefier, so that the down-wind legs could push back. Beefy steel catches more wind, increasing the force that's caus-ing the problem in the first place. Not only that but it demands more steel below to sup-port its weight. This feedback loop produced exponential jumps in the Steel Bill whenever anything got adjusted.

It wasn't long before someone pointed out that, from an aerodynamics standpoint, the tower was a horror show. Basically every strut and every cable was a cylinder—one of the draggiest shapes you can have. If we snapped an airfoil-shaped fairing around each of those cylinders, however, leaving it free to pivot into the wind, the drag went down by an order of magnitude and the Steel Bill dropped like—well, like a wrench dropped from the roof of a Top Click casino. And those fairings would have other benefits too; filled with lightweight insulation, they would reduce the thermal ups and downs caused by sunlight and direct exposure to space. The steel would live at a nice in-between temperature, not expanding and contracting so much, and brittleness would be less of a problem.

Everyone was feeling pretty satisfied with that solution when Carl raised an idea that, I suspect, some of the engineers had been hiding in their subsconscious and been afraid to voice: Why not fly the tower? If we were going to all the trouble to airfoilize everything, why not use the kind of airfoil that not only minimizes drag, but also produces lift?

Wings, in other words. The tower's lateral braces—the horizontal struts that joined its verticals together at regular intervals—would be enclosed in burnished-aluminum wings, actuated by motors that could change their angle of attack, trimming the airfoils to generate greater or lesser amounts of lift. When the jet stream played on the tower's upper reaches like a firehose slamming into a kid's Tinkertoy contraption—when, in other words, the maximum possible crush was being imposed on the downwind legs— the wings on that side would be trimmed so as to lift the whole thing upward and relieve the strain. Performing a kind of aerodynamic jujitsu, redirecting the very energy that would destroy the tower to actively hold it up. The tower would become half building, half kite.

People's understandable skepticism about that scheme had accounted for the need to maintain a huge empty swath downwind of it. Many took a dim view of a building that wouldn't stand up without continuous control system feedback.

When we had boarded the helirail, I'd exchanged a bit of small talk with Joe, the engineer sitting across from me. Then he had unrolled a big display, apologizing for hogging so much table space, and spent most of the journey poring over a big three-dimensional technical drawing—the servomechanism he was going to take a look at. My eyes wandered to it, and I noticed he was studying me. When I caught him looking, he glanced away sheepishly. "Penny for your thoughts," he mumbled.

"Oh, I spent years talking to concerned citizens in school gyms and senators in congressional hearings, selling them on this idea."

"Which idea?"

"Exactly," I said. "You've grown so used to it you don't even see it. I'm talking about the idea of flying the tower."

He shrugged. "It was going to require active damping anyway, to control oscillations," he said.

"'Otherwise, every slot machine on the Top Click will have to come equipped with a barf bag dispenser.' Yeah, I used to make a living telling people that. 'And from there it's a small step to using the same capability to help support the tower on those rare occasions when the jet stream is hitting it.'"

Joe was nodding. "There's no going back," he said. "It snuck up on us."

"What did?"

He was stumped for an answer and smiled helplessly for a moment. Then threw up his hands. "All things cyber. Anything with code in it. Anything connected to the Internet. This stuff creeped into our lives and we got dependent on it. Take it away and the economy crashes—just like the tower. You gotta embrace it."

"Exactly," I said. "My most vociferous opponent was a senator who was being kept alive by a pacemaker with a hundred thousand lines of embedded code."

Joe nodded. "When I was younger, I was frustrated that we weren't building big ambitious stuff anymore. Just writing dumb little apps. When Carl came along with the tower idea, and I understood it was going to have to fly—that it couldn't even stand up without embedded networks—the light went on. We had to stop building things for a generation, just to absorb—to get saturated with—the mentality that everything's net-worked, smart, active. Which enables us to build things that would have been impossible before, like you couldn't build skyscrapers before steel."

I nodded at the drawing in front of him, which had been looping through a little animation as we talked. "What's new in your world?"

"Oh, doing some performance tweaks. Under certain conditions we get a rumble in the tower at about one-tenth of a hertz— you might have felt it. The servos can't quite respond fast enough to defeat it. We're developing a workaround. More for comfort than for safety. Might force us to replace some of the control units—it's not something you can do by sitting on the ground typing." He nodded toward the luggage rack by the door where he had deposited a bright yellow plastic case, obviously heavy.

"That's okay," I said, "sitting on the ground typing wasn't Carl's style."

As if on cue the car dinged to warn us of impending deceleration. Joe began to collect his things. A minute later the car stopped in the middle of a sort of pod caught in the fretwork of the tower like a spider's egg case in a web. Lights came on, for it was deep dusk at this point. A tubular gangway osculated with the car's hatch, its pneumatic lips inflating to make an airtight seal. Air whooshed as a mild pressure difference was equalized, and my ears popped. The door dilated.

Joe nodded good-bye and lugged his bag case out into the station, which was a windowless bare metal tub. A minute later we were on our way again.

"I just wanted to introduce myself. Nicky Chu." This was the astronomer en route to the Top Click. "Sorry, but I didn't realize who you were until I heard your story."

"Have you spent much time up there, Nicky?"

"Just once, for orientation and safety briefings."

"Well, you're always welcome in the bar. We're having a little private observance tonight, but even so, feel free to stop in."

"I heard," Nicky said, and, perhaps in spite of herself, glanced toward the messenger bag. "I only wish I could have shared one of these rides with the man before…"

The pause was awkward. I said what Carl would have said: "Before he was incinerated in a giant kiln? Indeed."

A SENATOR HAD ONCE described the Internet as a series of tubes, which didn't describe the Internet very well but was a pretty apt characterization of the Top Click. "Shirtsleeves environment" had been the magic buzzword. I knew as much because Carl had once banned the phrase from PowerPoint slides—shortly before he had banned PowerPoint altogether, and then attempted to ban all meetings. "The Cape of Good Hope is not a shirtsleeves environment. Neither was the American West. The moon. The people who go to such places have an intrepid spirit that we ought to respect. I hate patronizing them by reassuring them it's all going to be in a shirtsleeves environment!"

This sort of rant had terminated some awkward conversations with casino executives and hoteliers. I had donated a small but significant chunk of my life to getting him to admit that my job would be easier and the Top Click would be more valuable if it had a breathable atmosphere that wouldn't cause simultaneous frostbite and sunburn. Building one big dome on the top was too inflexible, and we had ended up with a mess of cylindrical and hemispherical structures (because those shapes withstood pressurization) joined by tubular skybridges. The Top Click helirail terminal was a hemispherical dome, already awe-inspiring in a Roman Pantheon way even though it was just a shell. Radiating from it were tubes leading to unfinished casinos, hotels, office buildings, and the institute that Carl and some of his billionaire friends had endowed. The observatory was there, and that was where Nicky went after saying good-bye and exchanging contact data with me. I shouldered the bag with Carl in it and hiked down a tube to a lobby where I changed to another tube that took me to the First Bar in Space. Frog, the video producer, walked with me; having slept most of the way through the ride, he was in the mood for a drink. I helped him tow his luggage: a hard-shell case full of video gear and a Day-Glo pink backpack containing the parafoil he intended to use for the return trip.

It was a pretty small party. Carl didn't have a lot of friends. Alexandra, his daughter from a long-dead marriage, had flown in from London with her boyfriend, Roger, who was some sort of whizbang financial geek from a posh family. Tess was there to greet me with a glass of wine and a kiss. Our kids were off at college and at camp. Carl's younger brother Dave, a college volleyball coach, had come in from Ohio. He was already a little tipsy. Maxine, the CEO of Carl's charitable foundation, and her husband, Tom, a filmmaker. We took over one corner of the bar, which was pretty quiet anyway. Maria the bartender and Hiram, one of the regulars, were watching a Canadian hockey game on the big screen. Hiram, a teetotalling Mohawk ironworker, was knocking back an organic smoothie. Frog grabbed a stool at the other end of the bar, ordered a Guinness, whipped out his phone, and launched into a series of "you'll never guess where I'm calling from!" calls.

It was lovely to be home in my bar with my wife. I was just a few sips into that glass of wine, starting to wish that all of these nice guests would go away and leave us alone, when heads began to turn and I noticed that we had been joined by a woman in a space suit.

Not totally. Nicky Chu had had the good manners to remove the helmet and tuck it under her arm. She said, "Sorry, but I think we all need to get under cover. Or *over* cover is more like it."

"Over cover?" I asked.

Roger broke the long silence that followed. I don't know, maybe it was that British penchant for wordplay. "What's coming up from beneath?" he asked. "And how's it going to get through the floor?"

"High-energy gamma ray bursts," Nicky said, "and some antimatter."

"Antimatter?" several people said at once.

"I'll explain while you're donning," she said, and started backing toward the exit. "I'm afraid you're going to have to put down your drinks."

Donning, as most of us knew, meant putting on space suits. It was to living on the Top Click what the life vest drill was to an ocean cruise. Thanks to the space tourism industry, it had become pretty idiot proof. Even so, it did take a few minutes. They were stored in a vestibule, which for very sound reasons was a sealable windowless capsule. Nicky insisted we drag them out into an adjacent sky lobby—a future restaurant—with big west-facing windows. She wanted us to get a load of the storm.

And this bore no resemblance to watching a storm approach on the ground. We've all done that. From a distance you can look up into the structure of the high clouds, but as it gets closer all is swallowed in murk. Lightning bolts, hail, torrents of rain, and wind gusts jump out at you from nowhere.

Here, we were miles above the uppermost peaks of the anvil clouds, enjoying an unobstructed view of outer space. The Milky Way shot up like an angled fountain above the storm front, which from this height looked like a layer of ground-hugging dry ice fog in a disco. Sometimes it would glow briefly.

Nicky's warning had put me in mind of nuclear war and so I had to wait for my logical mind to catch up and tell me that those flashes were nothing more than lightning bolts, seen from above.

Nicky had turned toward me—but she wasn't looking at me. She was staring unfocused. "They're easiest to see in your peripheral vision," she remarked. "They'll be very high up—in space."

"What are you talking about?" Dave demanded. He wasn't handling this especially well. Fortunately Hiram interceded. "Sprites," he explained. "We see 'em all the time."

From anyone else this would have provoked a sarcastic rejoinder from Dave. Coming from a crag-faced, 250-pound Mohawk, it took on more gravity.

"Oh!" Tess exclaimed.

I heard the smile in Nicky's voice. "Big one there!"

"Where?" people were asking.

"It's already faded," Nicky said. But then I saw a disk of red light high up, which expanded while darkening in its center, becoming a scarlet halo before it winked out.

I turned back to Nicky to ask a question, which never made it out of my mouth as something huge registered in my peripheral vision: a cloud of red light, jellyfish-like, trailing hundreds of streaming filaments. By the time I had snapped my head around to focus on it, this had shrunk to a tiny blob that went dark.

Within a minute, everyone had witnessed at least one of these sprites and so all questions as to Nicky's credibility had gone away. For the most part they all faded in the blink of an eye. But sometimes, ghostly orbs of blue light would scamper up the red tendrils for a few moments afterward, prompting gasps of delight. These I heard over the wireless voice com system built into my suit—by this point I had my helmet on.

Nicky was watching their reactions uneasily, clearly wishing they would take this a little more seriously. "A couple of decades ago," she said, "some of our orbiting gamma ray observatories began picking up incredibly powerful bursts. Long story short, it became obvious that these were coming not down from deep space but up from *below*—from the earth. So powerful that they maxed out the sensors, so we couldn't even tell how massive they actually were. Turned out they were coming from thunderclouds. The conditions in those storm towers down there are impossibly strange. Free electrons get accelerated upward and get kicked up into a hyperenergetic state, massively relativistic, and at some point they bang into atoms in the tops of the storm towers with such energy that they produce gamma rays which in turn produce positrons—antimatter. The positrons have opposite charges, so they get accelerated downward. The cycle repeats, up and down, and at some point you get a burst of gamma rays that is seriously dangerous—you could get a lifetime's worth of hard radiation exposure in a flash." She paused for a moment, then stared directly at me with a crazy half smile. "The earth," she said, "is an alien world."

The story was jogging memories. This was one of those "gotchas" that had come along halfway through the project and precipitated a crisis for a few weeks. The hard part, actually, had been getting Carl and the other top decision makers to believe that it was for real. The engineering solution hadn't been that complicated—shield the floors of the buildings with radiation-stopping materials, and, during thunderstorms, evacuate any parts of the structure that hadn't been shielded yet—

"Thank you," I said, "you're a sharp one."

Nicky nodded.

"What is your idea? Why are we donning?" I asked her.

"There's a place over in the depot where some plate steel has been stacked up—I reckon if we huddle on top of that, it should stop most of the gamma rays coming up from the storm."

Roger had been listening intently to all this. In a weird burst of insight, I understood why: Alexandra was pregnant. She wasn't showing yet. So there was no real evidence to support my intuition. But she had declined the offer of a drink, which was unusual for her, and there'd been something in the way she and Roger looked at each other... Carl's grandchild was up here, taking shape in her womb. We had to get her over cover.

The depot that Nicky had spoken of was the old construction materials dump, near the middle of the Top Click. It was all out in the open, which was why we'd had to don in order to get there. In a few minutes' time we were all able to put on our helmets and let our suits run through their self-check routines. We stepped out into an airlock and experienced the weird sensation of feeling the suits stiffen around us as the outside pressure dropped. They were awkward to move in, and none of us was really trained in their use—they were for survival purposes only. For that reason a number of electrically powered scooters were parked in their charging docks right outside the exit. We merely had to waddle over to them, climb aboard, and then steer them away. In an ungainly queue we followed Nicky in a circuitous path among buildings-in-progress. Shortly we arrived at the depot and followed her to a place where corrugated steel floor panels had been stacked up in neat rectangular blocks almost as tall as our heads. Hiram, who of all of us was most adept at moving around in a suit, clambered up onto the top of a stack and then reached down to pull the rest of us after him.

The view here wasn't as good, but none of us doubted Nicky's judgment as to the gamma rays, so we didn't mind. Soon the most intense part of the storm was passing beneath us. We could tell as much from the fact that the red sprites were directly overhead. Most of us ended up lying on our backs so that we could gaze straight up and watch the light show.

We had taken all of these precautions for one reason: to avoid exposure to gamma radiation. The storm was nowhere near us. Far below, winds were buffeting the lower structure, but we didn't even feel it. Our view down blocked by tons of steel, our only clue that a storm was in progress was the sprites blooming tens of thousands of meters overhead.

All of which made the superbolt just that much more surprising.

Of course, we didn't know it was something called an "upward superbolt" until much later. At the time, I just assumed that I was dead for some reason, and that the transition to heaven, or hell, was a much more jarring event than what tended to be described by survivors of near-death experiences. My next hypothesis was that I was still alive, but not for long—I remember reaching up to touch my helmet, fearing that it had popped off. Nope, it was still there. Then, for a minute or two, I was convinced that terrorists had set off a small nuclear device somewhere on the Top Click. Buildings were damaged, debris—glowing hot—was cascading to the deck. Finally my ears recovered to the point where I could hear Nicky saying "lightning," and despite all of this chaos some part of my brain was registering the schoolgirlish objection that lightning was a cloud-ground interaction, and we were not between the clouds and the ground, so how could that be? Now, of course, I know more than I want to about upward superbolts: another fascinating middle-atmospheric phenomenon that Nicky hadn't gotten around to lecturing us about.

Shock and awe only last for so long and then you begin to take stock of reality.

The First Bar in Space was mostly gone. The superbolt had melted a hole through its floor and roof and it had explosively decompressed, vomiting its contents—barstools, dartboards, Carl's ashes—into space. So Nicky's precaution about the gamma rays had not only saved us from a stiff dose of radiation but, by dumb luck, kept us from being blown to bits and sprayed across the desert.

Several other buildings were no longer shirtsleeves environments. Some looked undamaged. Safety doors ought to have slammed down in the tube network, preventing depressurization of the whole Top Click. When the storm had passed and the danger of gamma rays was over, we'd move into one of the undamaged structures and wait for rescue.

In the meantime, we were in for a wild ride, because the tower had begun swaying and shuddering beneath us.

Panic would have been too obvious. I confess I was headed in that general direction, though, until Hiram's voice came through: "I don't care how big the lightning was," he said. "I rode that steel up and there is just no way it could have taken that much damage." He rolled off the stack of plates and let himself down to the deck. "I'm going to go have a look."

What the heck. My kid-having days were over. I had responsibilities. First and foremost to Carl's grandkid-in-the-making.

"Emma, what the *heck?!*" Tess called.

"The storm is over, baby," I said, and followed Hiram, who let me down easy to the deck.

Some touristy impulse led us straight to the wreckage of the First Bar in Space. We dropped to our knees and approached the hole in the deck on all fours.

Staring down through the hole, we could see, a couple of kilometers below us, something like a Venetian blind that had been attacked with a blowtorch. Several of those burnished-aluminum airfoils had been blasted by the superbolt. A huge strip of aluminum had peeled away from one of them and gotten wrapped around the one below it.

"Well, there's your problem," Hiram pronounced. "No wonder the tower ain't flying right." As if on cue, the structure lurched beneath us, eliciting squeals of horror from our friends back in the depot.

"Is it dangerous?" I asked him. Because one of the advantages of being a middle-aged chick in this world was the freedom to ask questions that a young male would be too insecure to voice.

"To people below? If some of that crap falls off? Sure!" he said. "To us? Nah. Structure's fine. Just ain't flying right. Only real risk is barfing in our helmets."

I wasn't about to second-guess Hiram, who had ridden the tower up from day one and had a strong intuitive feel for what made it stand up. But uneasy memories were stirring of briefings, years ago, about top-down failure cascades. The classic example being the Twin Towers, which had collapsed in toto despite the fact that all the initial damage had been confined to their upper floors. Debris from a high-level event could damage structural elements far below, with incalculable results. The thin, almost nonexistent atmosphere up here would allow debris to fall at supersonic velocity. Energy, and damage, would increase as the velocity *squared*...

Where was the problem, I wondered, that was preventing the tower from "flying right"? Had the superbolt fried the electronics? Jammed a mechanism? Bent a control surface?

Which caused me to remember one other detail from earlier in the evening...

"Crap," I said. "There's a guy down there. Working on the system. Joe. An engineer. I hope he's okay."

"I wonder if there's any way to reach him?" Tess asked. Reminding me that all of us up here were linked in a single conversation by a wireless mesh network.

"First things first," I said. "The absolute top priority is patrolling the edge of the Top Click to make sure no debris falls off the edge. Spread out and do that. If you see anything, report it to Hiram. Hiram, you'll have to jury-rig something..."

"I'll get a welding cart. Should be great for tacking things down."

"Everyone should be spreading out now," I insisted. "Storm's over, folks. I see clear air below, headed our way. Look for anything that might go over the edge, or get jostled loose by all this shaking. And while you're at it, look for buildings that are still pressurized, where we can take shelter before our suits run out of air."

"GOOD NEWS, BAD NEWS," Dave announced a minute later. "I found a little dome—a construction shack—that still has pressure. But this thing next to it got zapped real hard—it's about to shed a roof truss over the edge."

"I know the place. On my way," Hiram announced.

It didn't rain up here, so "roof" meant a piece of steel for reducing the flux of cosmic rays. The point being, a roof was a heavy object, and not something we wanted to drop off the top of the tower.

Toddling around in my suit, I caught sight of Hiram trundling a welding cart as fast as he could manage it. These carts weren't like terrestrial welders. They had built-in engines to generate power, fueled by liquid propane—but since there was little air up here, they also carried their own supply of liquid oxygen. It made an unwieldy package even for a big man like Hiram, but presently Dave waddled over to lend a hand.

Inside, our little refuge was like any other construction site office, decorated with free-bie catalogs from tool companies and beer posters featuring sexy babes. Once we got through the airlock and pulled off our helmets, we were able to sit down and take stock. Outside, Hiram was tack-welding the wayward truss into place, assisted by Dave and a contractor who had joined up with our little band. He'd been working late on the top floor of a casino when the lights had gone out and a six-foot-long arc had jumped out of a nearby faucet and connected with an electrical outlet, passing close enough to his head to singe his hair. Once we'd heard his story, we understood why we couldn't get Internet. But we could make cell-phone calls, connecting, albeit patchily, with towers on the ground.

Tess and Maria the bartender, who knew their way around the Top Click as well as anyone, swapped in new oxygen supplies and went out to reconnoiter for injured stragglers. I was able to get through on the phone to Joe's boss and hear the troubling, but hardly surprising, news that he hadn't checked in.

Which was how Roger, Frog, and I ended up abseiling three kilometers straight down the tower's central shaft on a rescue mission.

Why us three? Well, Frog was the veteran BASE jumper, a little past his prime and above his station, but—bottom line—the only way to prevent him from coming would have been to hit him on the head with a wrench and ziptie him to a girder. Roger, true to his pedigree, had mountaineering experience.

And I knew as much about the tower's weird little ins and outs as anyone.

The central shaft, which would one day be filled with some as-yet-unbuilt space launch tech, was empty. Ever-pragmatic construction workers had strung long cables down it, like mountaineers' ropes. They used mechanical descenders to glide down when they wanted to get lower but didn't have time to mess about with helirails. There were also elevators, but these had all shut themselves off when the superbolt had fritzed their electronics, and there seemed no way to reboot them without getting through to a customer service rep in Pakistan. Roger, the biggest member of our group, slung an extra space suit on his back (these folded up, sort of, into backpackable units, bulky but manageable). This was just in case Joe was in need of one. Hiram showed us how to harness the descenders to the outside of our suits. Each of us connected to a different cable—there were plenty of them—and then we backed off the rim of the shaft and let ourselves drop.

So this was a tubular vacancy, ten meters across and (currently) seventeen thousand meters long. Walking to the edge of it and looking straight down had become a popular tourist activity on the Top Click. To put this in perspective, it had the same relative dimensions as a forty-foot-long soda straw. As a rule, it was perfectly straight, as if it had been laser-drilled through a cube of granite. Quite a trick given that it was held in place by a wind-buffeted gas of metal.

Tonight, though, it was sashaying. You couldn't see the bottom from the top. It was like staring down the gullet of an undulating snake. Because, in Hiram's phrasing, the tower wasn't flying right. Its accustomed straightness was a process, not a state; it was made straight from one moment to the next by a feedback loop that had been severed.

As alarming as it looked, the undulation wasn't as huge as it appeared from above, and once we had adjusted the tension in our descenders, we were able to plunge more or less straight down. In a forty-foot soda straw, even a little bend looks enormous.

The self-weight of the cables became a problem after a while and so they terminated every hundred meters, forcing us to stop and transfer to new ones. It took us thirty transfers, and as many minutes, to get down to the altitude where Joe had detrained some hours ago.

This brought us into the Neck, the skinniest part of the tower, but in some ways the most complicated. The Top Click was destined to be the domain of gamblers and scientists. The bottom kilometers would be a city with an airport on its roof. The central core, a somewhat mysterious ballistics project. But the Neck was the domain of engineers: mechanical, control-system, and aeronautical. That's because it was here that the wind stress was at its peak, and here that it had to be addressed with what were called "active measures." The most conspicuous of these were the airfoils, large enough for people to walk around inside of them. At one level there was also an array of turbofan engines, the same as you see on airliners, which had been put there as a last-ditch measure in the event of a full-on jet stream hit. If that ever happened we would just fuel them up, turn them on, and run them full blast, thrusting back against the force of the wind, until the jet stream wandered away, a few hours or days later.

All of this gear for playing games with enormous forces had made the Neck beefier by far than the rest of the tower, and so as we descended silently into it, our view of the stars and of the curving horizon was interrupted, then cluttered, and finally all but blotted out by a mare's nest of engineering works, most of it wrapped in streamlined airfoils to make it less draggy.

At our target altitude, six horizontal braces radiated from the core to the six primary legs of the tower. These were trusses, webs of smaller members triangulated into rigid systems, looking a bit like radio towers laid on their sides. Plastic tubes had been built around them, forming airtight corridors.

Those in turn had been encased in aerodynamic sheaths. Six of those converged like spokes on the place where we stopped our descent and unhooked ourselves from the descenders. Moving deliberately, clipped to safety rails, leapfrogging from one handhold to the next—for the wind was fearsome—we made our way to the airlock that afforded entry to the southeastern strut/truss/tube/airfoil. Based on information from Joe's boss, I believed we would find him at the end of it. So I was dismayed when the airlock's control panel gave us the news that the tube was depressurized. This thing was supposed to be full of a proper atmosphere so that engineers could move along it without having to leave that all-important shirtsleeves environment. But apparently the superbolt had caused it to spring a leak. This was okay for me, Roger, and Frog, but I didn't know what it might portend for Joe.

In any case, opening the door was easy since we didn't have to cycle the airlock. We were confronted by a view down a straight tube a thousand meters long, illuminated dimly by blue LEDs. The steel truss had been equipped with plastic catwalk grating. We started walking. This would have been a lot easier in an atmosphere. As it was, I wished we'd had some of those electric scooters, like on the Top Click. The designers of those suits had made the best of a tough design challenge, but at the end of the day they were made for passive survivors awaiting rescue by people in real space suits. Hiking down a catwalk wasn't in the design spec. It was like wading through wet cement and feeling it start to harden whenever you planted a foot. I wanted to break the mood with a joke about what great cardio this was, but I was too out of breath, and judging from the sound effects in my headphones, Roger and Frog weren't doing much better.

I was about ready to start whining about how hard it all was when we got to the end of the tube—meaning we had reached the southeastern Primary—and walked through another dead airlock into the pod where Joe had been working.

The pod was spherical. A floor and a ceiling had been stretched across it to turn it into a round room about the size of a two-car garage. The dome-shaped spaces above and below were packed respectively with electronics and with survival gear. The first thing I noticed when I walked in was an open floor hatch, which gave me hope that Joe had had time to yank it open and grab a suit.

But Joe wasn't in here.

My eye was drawn to a scarlet flash on the other side of the darkened room. I realized I was looking straight out through a hole that had been blasted in the spherical shell. The red flash had been one of those sprites, off in the distance, high above the top of the thunderstorm as it migrated eastward.

Frog bent down and picked up an overturned swivel chair. Its plastic upholstery was patchy where it had melted and congealed.

On the workspace where Joe had been seated, and on the jagged twists of metal around the rupture, was a mess that I couldn't identify at first—because I didn't want to. And when I did, I almost threw up in my suit. Joe hadn't opened the floor hatch, I realized. It had been blown open when this whole pod had explosively decompressed. The atmosphere had blasted out the hole, taking Joe with it. Later forensic analysis suggested he'd been killed instantly by the superbolt, so at least he'd been spared the experience of being spat out, fully conscious, into free fall. But none of that changed the fact that, through no fault of his own, he'd been sitting in the wrong place at the wrong time. He had become the third accidental fatality on the tower construction project. Number one had been early—a forklift mishap, moving some steel around. Number two had been only a couple of months ago: a taut cable had been snapped by a wayward crane; the broken end recoiled under tension and struck a worker hard enough to break his neck. Joe was number three, killed instantly by an upward superbolt: a species of upper-atmosphere monster of which we had known only traces and rumors when the tower had been designed.

What we did next got described all wrong in the news reports. Oh, they weren't factually incorrect, but they got the emotional tenor wrong. Yes, seeing that the southeastern control node had been blitzed off the network, we concluded that its responsibilities would have to be shunted to other nodes on the same level that still had luxuries such as power and atmosphere. Lacking communication with the ground, we had to make do with a few erratic cell-phone conversations. Roger, Frog, and I spread out to the south, northeast, and north control nodes on the same level—lots more cardio—and finally took those cursed suits off and, following instructions from the ground, repatched cables and typed in arcane computer commands until control had been transferred. The tower stopped swaying and, as the control loops recalibrated to its new aerodynamics, stopped vibrating as well. All of that was true. But the news feeds described it as an Apollo 13 type of crisis, which it never was. They made it sound like we were doing really cool, difficult work under pressure, when in reality most of it was sitting in shirt-sleeves (sorry, Carl!) and typing. And they totally failed to understand the context and the tone that had been set by the death of Joe.

The one thing they got right was what happened in the wee hours that followed: Hiram and Frog going out on the damaged airfoil to corral loose pieces of metal that were banging around in the wind and that could have inflicted catastrophic damage had they come loose. That was really dangerous work, performed at great personal risk without proper safety lines and, because it took longer than expected, with dwindling air supplies and cold-numbed digits. Frog, true to BASE-jumper tradition, went out the farthest, and took the biggest risks—maybe because he had a parasail strapped to his back.

And, though he later denied it, I think he had a plan. Only after all of the loose debris had been securely lashed and tack-welded down did he "fall off" in an "unexpected wind gust" and free-dive for a few thousand meters before deploying his parasail and enjoying a long ride down to terra firma. You've seen the YouTube of him touching down in the desert at dawn, popping off his helmet, gathering up his chute, and striding toward the camera to make the grim announcement that a man had died up on the tower last night. Standing there in his space suit, unshaven, exhilarated by his "fall" but sobered by the grisly scene he'd witnessed in the pod, he looked like nothing other than an astronaut.

And an astronaut he was, on that morning. One without a rocket. Exploring, and embracing the dangers, not of outer space but of the atmosphæra incognita that, hidden from earthlings' view by thunderheads, stretches like an electrified shoal between us and the deep ocean of the cosmos.

STORY NOTES

NEAL STEPHENSON

The Tall Tower idea is based on papers written by Geoffrey A. Landis ("Compression Structures for Earth Launch," 1998) and Landis and Vincent Denis ("High Altitude Launch for a Practical SSTO," 2003). In addition, the author is grateful to Keith D. Hjelmstad of Arizona State University for many illuminating discussions of the structural ramifications; Ed Finn and Michael Crow, also of ASU, for fostering Project Hieroglyph and the Center for Science and the Imagination; and Daniel MacDonald, Jenny Hu, and Kevin Finke for their participation in further analysis of the tower idea. The idea of using engines to push back against jet stream events should be credited to Jeff Bezos. Finally, Gregory Benford's enthusiasm for the idea and the story are noted with warm appreciation.

STRUCTURAL DESIGN OF THE TALL TOWER

KEITH D. HJELMSTAD

Read a technical paper about the structural design of the Tall Tower by Keith D. Hjelmstad of Arizona State University at hieroglyph.asu. edu/tall-tower.